CW00932522

Celi... y

Sebastian

The Logophile Edition

Aisling Geraghty

Celina & Sebastian

Copyright © 2024 by Aisling Geraghty

All Rights Reserved

For Catriona

1966~2018

Acknowledgements

The author wishes to thank Iza and Marley, who provided the delightful illustrations of Celina and Sebastian. A *merci beaucoup* to Hubert and Pipa for their backing. Appreciation to all the team at Amazon Publishing especially Solomon Elias and Audrey Hope for encouraging independent writers. 'If you're not prepared to be wrong, you'll never do anything meaningful' is an adaptation of a quote from the educationalist Sir Ken Robinson. The wisdom of Robert Frost, Emily Dickinson, Rudyard Kipling, Alfred, Lord Tennyson and J Krishnamurti makes a cameo appearance. This book cover and a number of symbolic images throughout the publication have been designed using the generous and skilled assets available at Freepik.com.

Disclaimer

This is a work of fiction from the author's imagination. Any events or characters baring any resemblance to real life situations or people are purely coincidental. The author bears no liability for what the reader may or may not choose to do or say as a result of reading this piece of fiction.

Table of Contents

Foreword

I wrote this in service to adolescents who already enjoy reading. I have taught them for many years now.

This book invites them to escape back into their imaginations, if only for a book.

To contribute a new facet to the selection of reading material for young adults was worth some effort. When we look at the available market material, it predominantly focuses on the now and the future potential of their lives. It also focuses on getting non-readers to start reading, perhaps neglecting the avid reader who needs more of a challenge.

Few examples focus on asking them to look back over the hill, at that vast expanse that was their childhood imagination, or to run back into it wildly and embrace the child they still are. We forget they are still children.

With the greatest respect, I am passionate about the dialogue included here and happily include diluted profanities like 'arse', 'feck' or 'shite'. Too much of their lives are already sterilised of authenticity.

There are over 270,000 words in the Oxford English Dictionary. Circa 171,000 of them are in regular use. This means that every child born into the English language has the ability to access a huge store of richness in expression – profanities included. Most of us go through life not realising each word of English is ours to spend *ad Infinium*.

I have always wanted to write a piece of creative fiction for adolescents that did not tell its readers how many words they could own at a particular age and time in their lives. In attempting to organise, officiate, and evaluate reading patterns and literacy amongst the young and get them to read more, we have, in my opinion, removed the very thing that would get them *to want to read* more – the wilderness of a good measure of unknown vocabulary. We may have sterilised them out of their own natural desire to explore. It is as though through giving ourselves jobs or feeling validated ourselves, we have mowed a track through that wilderness and asked them to see the joy *only on either side* of a pre-carved pathway. We are guilty of *analysis paralysis* in typeface.

So, this is it, hopefully just one of the heart-warming shooting stars that are the remains of their childhood exploding above their heads. Take your scythe people, we're going feral to hack down words in 3D…are *you coming?*

The French Stare

It was thirteen minutes past ten o'clock in the French village of St Joseph d'Andaines when an at first indistinguishable bird flew low by the church belfry. The suppression of unfamiliar dead heat meant the Hegarty family were only just beginning to stir for breakfast in their *maison secondaire*.

Sebastian had been up since the clamour of church bells at seven am. It shook his skull stupid, as it did every morning. All the two legs had been flopping around from couch to chair to bed since they arrived. They could often be seen waving bits of paper, cardboard, in fact anything flat they could find in front of their faces. For whatever

1

reason unknown to Sebastian; they couldn't or
wouldn't pant. Eventually,

they would settle down as
the days wore on and they
had   no   problem
whatsoever with the seven
am   wake-up   call,   they
continued not to heed it. Sebastian thought their
inability to hear it could have something to do with
their poor design. You see, they had two big legs
and then two stumpier legs higher up. Either way,
he kept an eye on the house and garden when all
the two legs were at slumber. It was a natural
appointment.

The heat of the day was still and searing, and
Sebastian took a strategic position under the peach
tree with its many branches. There she was again.
The bird came by through the left portion of the
garden with a body density that seemed a little too
much for its given wing support. Such was the
plight of the country bird, Sebastian thought; the
pickings were plentiful. Despite the odds of getting

airborne not looking too good, Sebastian was impressed that the bird had adapted to what was clearly an impediment of sorts and had achieved a well-accomplished style. She (he had decided 'it' was a she, for, despite the cumbersome nature of her flight, there was something feminine at play in her movements) had landed on the garden wall and Sebastian noticed something unusual about her feathers, there was no separation in them. The bird was knitted. A chunky and super tight garter stitch in slate grey. He knew about these things because Jackie two legs knitted with her two stumpier legs all the time but had yet to produce anything wearable. He was torn between trying to process what he was seeing and stepping out to chase the thing clear off the garden wall. He knew the garden wall meant that what was inside it belonged to him; walls are walls. You see, in truth, Sebastian didn't understand that France and Ireland were two different land masses, he just knew that in between being in one place and the other, he felt very queasy indeed.

3

Now before I continue, I'd like to introduce you to the concept of a Walla Walla because this is where our story is going. The Walla Walla is a unique union here in France between a dog and a duck. Dogs and ducks have a lot in common. They both love food, they are all business when they walk, they are loyal and territorial ~ and they sometimes take the odd nip! But we won't say too much about that because they are generally very good, and they only do it for protective reasons anyway, not out of wanton badness.

Deep in the Andaines Forest between South Normandy and the Pay de la Loire, the Walla Walla was first sighted over four hundred years ago and it is here they have continued to flourish. They are now as commonplace as the protected peregrine falcons. Magic happens in the countryside all over the world, and the French are so open-minded and protective of creative ways of being, that they never mention the phenomenon for fear it will in some ways threaten its existence.

So, down to the nitty gritty. This is how the

Walla Walla happens. The duck looks to make a union of souls (what the Irish call your *Anamchara*) with a willing dog. When the two agree to the terms and conditions of their arrangement, it is followed by a special ritual, like a ceremony, sort of like a wedding, but not that kind of love. The duck perches itself on the dog's neck with a little extra weight on the left shoulder. If the dog is okay with the feel of it all, then the union is sealed with a thrilling run through the vastness of the forest floor. As the snags, thistles, thickets, and dry wooded forest floor threaten to halt their fun, both animals reach far into their throats and free every single sound in their repertoire – thundering through – nothing can stop them – they believe it, and so it is. The trees act like covetous allies, buffering, blanketing, and returning the cacophony as though it were a mere squeak. The purpose of this union is simple, it is to not feel so alone in the world, to know that you will matter to your *Anamchara* or Walla Walla on a level away from ordinary day-to-day life.

Celina was the bird's name, and she never became part of a Walla Walla because she was too heavy. This was not a judgement by any of the dogs she met, they had all been very obliging in trying to make a Walla Walla happen. This was simply a literal physical fact. She had failed to meet a dog who could carry her without doing themselves an injury. That was, until she clapped eyes on Sebastian.

There was something different about this dog, he struggled in the heat, he was large and super hairy, and his barks were full of bravado, but she knew his weaknesses, for she felt them herself. The energy and sounds at his house were unlike anything she was used to hearing or feeling. She thought that like some of her bird friends, he may need to migrate south, though she thought that unlikely as he could hardly handle the heat here as it is, and she couldn't see his two legs flock practising for a journey anywhere when they came to stay, they just did a lot of lolling around. Perhaps he migrated north in some way? There was only one way to find out, she settled into the abundance of ivy that platted his garden walls and waited for him to make eye contact.

Two Legs - Four Legs

Sebastian refused to return eye contact and was shocked at the affront posed by this bird; he knew French flies were cheeky, but he didn't know it extended to everything with wings. He got her coordinates through his peripheral vision and wandered towards that section of the garden as though she didn't exist at all.

That's MY wall.

He muttered to himself (in doggery). Thoroughly vexed he was.

When he got within a few yards of her perch, he didn't quite know what to do, so he barked in a volley of aimless munition, it circled up into the air above and around his head. No move.

Celina watched as a blond two legs came out of the back door with food that looked like it was for a dog.

Sebastian, dat's de boy! Good fella – housh my big fella? Oh, he's a big fella doin' big fella tings.

At that moment Sebastian's body transformed and transfigured up through the garden like a polar bear attempting to perform Swan Lake. His entire body was swathing to the tune of this foreign tongue. Celina knew enough about dogs to know that nothing comes between them and their food – so she left. For now.

What was that? I must have frightened it off.

By and by, the remaining two legs came through the back doors in various states of waking, all had time to greet Sebastian, and each other – though he seemed to be more important than anyone else. It's a good job two legs provide such abundant food, it helps the likes of Sebastian look past them being up on their hind legs like that with two little stumpy things doing all the fidgeting up higher—it's enough to make your stomach ill looking at them. There was blond two legs who was called Jackie, she was always very busy. Grey two legs who was called Sean, he was not always very busy. Brown two legs who was called Millie, she always seemed to be looking for *la mot juste*! She was a very officious character altogether. Then there was a grumpy two legs, I can't define this one by hair because it needed a wash and a cut, so I might get the shade wrong. Their name was Raven. Had Celina hung around long enough she would have seen that Sebastian was really just a two legs with four legs.

The Full Irish

By day five of their settling-in period, they were beginning to acclimatise to the heat. An exciting procession of foods came from the foraging heaven that was the interior of the Hegarty family den: fried eggs, cold orange juice, sizzling sausages, crispy rashers, warm toast, soft real butter, hot tea & fresh milk. When all was settled, various exchanges between the two legs cris-

crossed the table, even Raven two legs got industriously involved in the passing, buttering, and pouring.

Sebastian nosed the air with varying degrees of interest, his nostrils flared most alarmingly when the scent of sausages was carried on the mild morning breeze. It was carried right to the heart of his lungs, where it belonged. He sat with the family and drew attention to himself by how oddly observant he was. They joked about him good-naturedly and everyone took their opportunity to rub him, each with their own particular way of doing it. Sean two legs did it proudly, Jackie two legs always squished her body against him and changed her way of speaking completely, she sounded like a two legs just learning to talk. Raven two legs petted him conspiratorially. Mille two legs greeted Sebastian as though she was having a working breakfast with a colleague.

Sean two legs had a breakfast ritual which involved buttering a slice of bread and cutting half a sausage, he would then perch both on the side of his plate. A change occurred in Sebastian's temperament when this happened, he knew his place at the table was now validated and the pride between them was unspoken and reciprocated. Jackie two legs never gave him any of her food, yet, in the main he seemed to follow her around like a puppy dog more than he did any of the rest of them. Her energy was the tune to which this flock vibrated – she was the *head honcho*, even if she was a little tight when it came to sharing her food. Her contribution was broader.

As the meal was nearing an end, Jackie two legs asked Raven two legs to hose down the dog, to which he replied:

-    *I'm busy.*

For someone who claimed to be busy so often, I never actually saw him do anything except go from sun lounger to hammock and perhaps for a long walk alone.

-    *Doing what?*
-    *Stuff. I've got to phone Arson back home;*

13

he thinks he might be adopted, and he's really upset about it.

- *Who's this Arson is again? Is it Emily, John's young one, sure she's the spittin' image of John, what's she on about??*

- *That's his dead name mum, don't use it again.*

That was the end of that then, the whole family seemed to know that any further enquiry would not end well. He was cajoled into removing a few dishes from the breakfast table and that would have to be enough for now. He walked towards the house to go and sleep off breakfast for a bit. The groggy aimless rebellion of a morning teenager was complete with his final stroke; a whole rasher under the table to Sebastian before he left. Sebastian kept the munching low key. An affectionately aggressive rub of the dog's head, tongue clenched between his teeth – Raven two legs' social life was now over, until teatime.

Millie buttered a slice of toast and put her

mother's home-made white cherry jam on it, the garden had three white cherry trees and the jam became a sweet staple at the house. She took the toast to her room to work on her latest impassioned plea for a rethink on the international template for schooling.

Jackie and Sean two legs remained at the table. Now it was time for the breakfast ritual. Sean two legs was unaware that Raven had already given a sample of the morning's offering to Sebastian. Sebastian never let on and sat upright. He looked ever so intelligent in this pose. He licked his lips, tucked in his chin, gave the paw, gave the two paws, stood like a two legs, and basically ruined the whole ceremonial routine with overexcitement. Sean two legs encouraged composure, and off they went again. This time it went off like a dream: butter reworked into the bread and swiped on the sides was met by Sebastian's eyes palpably focused, and his body bolt erect – if he could have saluted, he would have – this was going to go off without a hitch. The bread and sausage were removed from the plate in that order and gently, slowly, stylishly they were handed over. Sebastian (despite his nature) modestly took the bread as though he really daren't, his acting skills on this occasion were supreme. The beautifully buttered bread melted down his throat with minimal chewing. He only chewed it at all because Sean two legs would tell him off over a single gulp. He had once swallowed a tennis ball whole thinking it was an apple and had to have it surgically removed, Sean two legs went on and on for an age about the expense of stupidity. The sausage part of the ritual always proved a little harder to pull off: it took all his strength to appear graceful and on more than one occasion during my observations – he almost didn't make it. But not this time, mission complete.

The next ritual I observed was the afterparty. This is where the intangible link between Jackie two legs and her dog managed to move me. She would pour herself a fresh cup of tea and return to her seat, table cleared, it was just her and

Sebastian and boy did he love it. She spoke her special language that she seemed to reserve only for him. I was glad I didn't have to tell her that he didn't understand a word of it.

- *Who ish da big fella? You ish da big fella. Oh, he is de best fella ever was, oh yesh he is…hesh de best fella…he is a big scardy fella, oh yesh he is. He gonna be out in de garden and he shes de birdy and he barkin' like a big fella but hesh a big shcardy fella.*

You can see where it goes from here, probably fifteen to twenty minutes of the same, coupled with rubs and hugs and kisses – just the two of them. She had a way of petting his head that pealed back his entire eye socket and made the top of his head look as if it had been hit with a mallet. He looked shocked, happy, and scared all at once. The family often told her off over it, but she said she couldn't help herself. Her food for him was love, and he missed her badly whenever she went off to forage. Though he was confident of her success at foraging, he worried about her if she returned even ten minutes later than usual, and he kept watch at the front room window from which he had to keep an eye on no less than three possible return routes. It was not a job he felt; it was a duty he was proud to perform.

As a habit, Millie two legs would make Sebastian sit in her room while she spoke to him as though he was a member of a much wider audience. Like most teenagers worth their salt, Mille wanted to set humanity straight on a few things and she would start by addressing Sebastian, a neutral audience, before she exposed her pleas to the more public critics who would decide that her cause was or wasn't worth their attention. She had joined Greta Thunberg's school strike not just for the *climate* but for the fact that she felt schooling as a concept had lost its way. Greta was missing nothing.

Physically, Millie took after her father, a tall, elegant man whose body was upright when upright and a snapping flow of angles when seated. Cool and still, her presence inspired confidence, but she was only sixteen, and her mind needed to catch up with her body. She was, as yet, too emotionally delicate to share her convictions with even the possibility of a negative critic, so for now she was only interested in preaching to the converted.

Sebastian had no idea what she was talking about of course, but he could tell from a feeling he had inside himself that it was important to her, so he stayed where she asked him to stay. She always spoke with the windows open, the freedom of speaking fluent English loudly in a French village where few could understand what she was saying felt liberating, she relished the anonymity of it.

Raven two legs said that it was interfering with his international human rights to have such white noise invading his space so regularly. Invariably this ended in Raven two legs removing Millie's one audience member and taking him on a long walk through an undisclosed forest he found some three kilometres away.

Raven two legs was named Cian when he was born, however today he preferred to go by the name Raven. He was going through the mother of all hormonal rollercoasters since the onset of his adolescence, and it was taking its toll on him and everyone around him. His family gave him a wide berth at times.

At school one or two teachers were not so understanding. His least favourite teacher almost had him put in detention for 'insubordination' (who even uses that word anymore) when he pointed out the correct way to pronounce her name. Mrs Mahony could spin her head three hundred and sixty degrees according to Raven and most of his peers, and although her name was Irish, she wasn't. Rather than respect hundreds of years' worth of pronunciation history, she became one of those people who decided that a name needed a fresh approach – so she pronounced it Mrs *Ma HONE EE* instead of *MAHoney*. She must have thought it gave her some sort of extra flair, so it caused quite the giggle in class when he pointed out on behalf of his ancestors:

- *You're pronouncing it wrong. It's **MAHoney,** not **Ma HONE EE.** Phonetically Ma HONE means 'my arse' in Irish.*

Although the pronunciation bit was true it earned him a strong telling off for being disrespectful, no mention of the disrespect to the name.

The truth is, Raven couldn't stand the two-faced nature of people in any walk of life, the worlds they created for themselves, the narrative they decided was their life, when the reality of both were clear for everyone else to see. It was disheartening to him that a grown adult would think that by putting a slant on their surname, they themselves would be somewhat different. Adults were supposed to inspire them, and yet few of them had grown up themselves, he felt.

He discussed these issues at length with Sebastian on their peaceful and leisurely walks through the forest he and Sebastian frequented.

21

Sebastian's only job it seemed was to accompany him and try to make him take life less seriously; but how, when there were so many MaHON EEs about?

Today the thirst of the long grass which had succumbed to the heat had cushioned their footsteps. It was thirty-two degrees, and it was 1:30 pm. They walked *a purpose* to get into the cool of the forest as soon as they could. The harvest was over and there was wholescale desolation in the fields, save for a few pastures given over to corn. Raven did not think he would be lucky enough to encounter the stag he saw there last year, but not only did he see him again, he saw his doe too. In fact, the doe seemed to see him as she momentarily stopped stripping the riper foliage and produce from a blackberry bush. She continued eating unperturbed – perceiving Raven to be no threat. Raven loved this, he knew he was not a problem and so did nature.

They sat by the stream that provided a barrier between them and the stag with his doe. The soft methodical sound of the water had them both loving life in that time, in that place, with absolutely nothing to do and all day to do it.

-   *Sebbie, take a drink. Good boy.*

Meanwhile Sean two legs was looking out of the sitting room window inquisitively. Occasionally, he checked with the others how long Raven and Sebastian were gone. He was a retired Garda sergeant who had not lost his suspicion of foul play. Every move the family had made, since his retirement, became a cause for concern to him. Since his retirement it had come to his attention that his wife Jackie had enhanced her bohemian qualities over the years while he was at work. He knew she was thoroughly reckless with the hub caps on her car wheels, not to mention the car's bodywork - but she had gotten rather feckless with other important matters too, in his opinion. He felt he had retired just in time to do something about it. All the family suggested he get himself a hobby. He said he didn't have time now that he realised how much help the family needed just to stay in one piece. Retirement had brought about a number of ailments for Sean, not least of which were meddling in everyone's business, and labouring points of advice until the arse fell out of them.

But when it came to Sebastian, he stopped being annoying. He was grateful, proud, even humbled to own such a beautiful dog. He always wanted to bring him everywhere to soak up the compliments he would receive, not in an egotistical way – you see, this was the way Sean expressed love. He would proudly repeat the compliments to all the family even though they had heard them all themselves.

- *OMG look at that dog, he's a bear!*
- *Did you hear that on the ship's deck Jackie? She was a lovely lady wasn't she?*
- *Oh, he's gorgeous, can I pet him…what is he…a St. Bernard? Said she.*
- *No, he's a Bernese Mountain Dog, says I.*

They always get those two mixed up!

Sean shook his head good humouredly.

- *No, remarkably…he doesn't actually eat as much as you'd think.*

Sean would add unprompted.

- *WE KNOW DAD, WE WERE THERE!*

Millie shouted in a rare outburst of intolerance (which she always hated herself for afterwards).

- *Sorry, sorry.*

Sean two legs just loved Sebastian in a man's way: awkward but sincere.

As for Sebastian himself? He couldn't be happier, he felt loved, he felt valued, and he felt an inexorable part of the family. He briefly remembered having another family when he was younger that looked a lot more like him, but that was a long time ago and he wished them well wherever they were. He hoped they were living their best lives, just like him.

Everyone needed him and it's nice to feel needed. It was catching, because that night – plumped up comfortably on the garden wall; the duck had returned, and she also seemed to be in need of him.

Bonsoir Mon Ami

- *Pst…*
- *Pst…*

All French ducks knew how to speak doggery because of their Walla Walla arrangements. She had an accent, but the words were identifiable.

- *Pst...* she said a little sharper this time.
- *Hey…Sebastian, my name is Celina. Don't look away. I know you can see me, and you can understand me because I am speaking to you in doggery. Look this way, Sebastian.*

That night the dank hothouse of an inland summer night breathed its stifling low mist across Sebastian's fur and trailed itself on through the

27

lawn. Petrichor rose in such dense abundance after just the lightest of showers, though its smell was divine, it brought only minimal relief to the atmosphere. The oppressive warmth was beginning to bear down on Sebastian's temperament, and he was most certainly discombobulated. Sebastian stared straight at Celina with his big mutton head. He couldn't believe his ears. He thought for a moment he might be in a lucid dream caused by the heat.

It seemed not even the slugs could continue their measured journey with any great conviction in this heat. Sebastian could see creatures he could not name, creatures that have no winter lives. Mossy spores of humidity intercepted his breathing and caused it to react in shallowness. He loved it here; it terrified and thrilled him in equal measure. He felt at once truly alive and in immediate peril almost daily; it exhilarated him, and never was that more true than at this moment. He was being addressed by a duck who was wearing a jumper.

- *How can you talk to me?*
- *In France, dogs and ducks have a lifelong relationship; they talk duckery, and we talk doggery. The language of ducks and dogs is internationally understood by both. There is no variation on the language itself save for a slight accent or a colloquialism here and there.*
- *Why?*
- *Nobody knows why, other than the fact that it feels right. During a duck's lifetime (once they are fully independent) they will go in search of a dog to call his or her own.*
- *Who's your dog?*

A rogue breeze whipped up out of nowhere around their ankles, flustered about their bodies like an inconsolable and irate child, bet them around the head a little and then barrelled off over the fields in search of some more victims. Celina lost her footing on the wall, and it was a painful sight. At first, she tried to pretend it wasn't

29

happening, she pleaded internally, silently, vibrationally with every fibre of her webbed feet. The transfer of unspoken mortified instructions shot back and forward from one foot to the other, the microscopic twisting of skin and sinew were all to no avail – this was not water, and she could not hide her paddling panic, it was a done deal. She was going to fall.

The fall was in one fell dump. An airless, graceless dollop, wallop, or fallop as ducks were in the habit of calling it. She fell a distance from Sebastian's feet and mercifully landed facing away from him. She lay there in stunned acceptance of the fall. This gave her a small amount of time to come up with a plan. A very small amount of time, for as sure as wind is rain Sebastian came sniffing. He had a vast nose, each nostril a tunnel of moisture and breath. His bulk was substantial. She played unconscious, but his outward breaths were lifting her head feathers ever so slightly and were in danger of making her emit the tiniest tickled wheeze. He was close, spacial awareness was not a gift Sebastian possessed. She held tight. Thankfully, Sebastian sat down and just waited for signs of life. After a few minutes when she had collected herself, she flopped sideways, wings akimbo and said:

- *I'm alright.*
- *Why did you do that?*
- *I didn't 'do that' Sebastian, the wind did it.*

She was now fully on her back and instructed Sebastian to do the same as though the whole fall had sped up a convenient prior decision for them to look at the stars. She tried to adapt Jackie two legs' voice because he seemed to like it so much, she didn't know how successful she would be – it was hard enough to speak doggery as it was. To her amazement, he did what he was told and rolled on his back. The whole sight above him made him feel faint in a wonderful way. Beyond, there lay a torrential mass of stars in a remote firmament over him. The scale was supersized compared to what he was used to seeing. He felt like those people he'd heard Millie talk about one evening. There are two legs who are afraid of physically large things, and he was beginning to feel like one of them now.

"Go inside!" was the reminder from the woodpigeon's reassuring coos and gobbles. *"Go inside!"* Before the moths detect the light and annoy you with their constant fluttering in the dining room all night, or as Jackie would say,

- *Go inside before some of the wilder accessories of the French country night air frighten the bejasus out of you Sebastian.*

- *He'll take off up over that wall someday Jackie with the fright, you know what he's like, and sure, I can't speak a word of French in order to get help. You'll be balling your head off and no amount of words English or French will be coming out of you. You've had your warning, all of you. Don't come running to me when he does it. I wish you'd all listen to me.*

Sean was a great man for making catastrophic predictions about the family from the comfort of whatever armchair he seemed to claim as his own. And it didn't stop with the welfare of Sebastian. If the family had listened to him on a whole host of potential founderings, they'd never have put one foot in front of the other and they'd barely have breathed in and out in many a year, had they taken him seriously. Jackie two legs on the other hand was a dreamer and many of her dreams had come true, though she was often quietly thankful for Sean's outlook when she dreamed a dream too far.

Sebastian decided to get up and return to the family. He realised he felt dizzy when he got up and began to stagger forward and sideways as he got to grips with this new kind of feeling. He steadied himself. Sebastian's train of thought remained unexplained to Celina. And that's the way they continued to roll naturally as time went on. They could have their own thoughts, *pas de problèm.*

Celina smirked, the conversation of power was

taking place between them and the first hurdle of becoming a Walla Walla had been successful; a *fair exchange of unspoken truths between two equals.*

- *Sebastian, where are you going?*
- *Inside.*
- *But I haven't shown you how to be with me as a Walla Walla.*
- *What's that? Have you not got a French dog for that...whatever it is?*

Celina flushed with humiliation; dippy and all as Sebastian could be, he knew when someone needed rescuing.

- *I'll do it. I think. How do I do it?*
- *Okay, so. Come over here and I will hop on the back of your neck, and I will lean in a little heavier on the left leg.*
- *Why?*
- *Why what?*
- *Why a little heavier on the left leg?*

- *Something to do with keeping creativity alive.*

The advantage of Sebastian's size was that she was sure he could carry her. The disadvantage was mounting him. A little wing work was necessary with this one, it would be tricky.

- *One, two, three, HOOPa…*

No joy. She had fluttered all the way from the left to the right side of him and down again. She ran around the front of him to the starting position again.

- *What can I do to help?*
- *I don't know, the contours of your body are hard to distinguish.*
- *You know, there is a shaved part of my fur from the back of my ears to the front of my chest on both sides? Jackie does it every time we come here so that when I turn my head sideways, I will feel the breeze hit my skin directly. You can't see it unless I*

35

actually turn my head sideways – see? She
also gives me what she calls a Brazilian so
that I can feel the benefit of the tiled floor
when I sit down. She's a cracker.

- *That's useful, so if I just land on the top, my*
  legs and feet will just slide into the groove
  on both sides if I feel for the track? Let's try
  that.

Celina hovered above Sebastian's neck and shoulders, centred herself, landed, and her legs found the track in the coat on both sides. At first the physical intimacy of leg on short fur was unusual. In time it became like a second skin for both of them and they weren't uncomfortable at all about the nearness of it.

She tapped him with both legs and said that that was one of the commands to move forward. She told him the more rapidly she tapped, the faster she expected him to go.

- *Let me explain something to you Celina*
  about my relationship with power and

*speed. I'm a Bernese Mountain Dog, my
kind were bred for pulling carts. Not all
dogs were bred with equal abilities. So, in
short, I have large bursts of unbridled
energy and strength followed by a flop out.
That's the way I am.*

- *Right. We can work around that then.*

As they walked aimlessly around the garden
together, she used her wings to stroke the top of
his head in thanks. The soft nature of the feathers
was something new to Sebastian, considering
Jackie always pulled the head off him with similar
moves. So, she began to explain the use of her
wings in the Walla Walla setting: a wing stroke on
the left ear was 'go left' and a wing stroke on the
right ear was 'go right' and a wing stroke on both
at the same time was 'stop' – and finally her wings
pressing down hard on both ears was 'go forward,'
and that along with her foot tapping should
increase his speed.

- *Clear enough Sebastian? Or can I call you*

Sebbie?

- *I'll respond to both, so I really don't mind.*

She had heard his name being reduced to Sebbie once or twice when she was within ear shot of the house that day (which was more often than she cared to admit). A nickname I think they call it.

Celina told him the story of the Walla Walla tradition in France which originated close by, in the Andaines Forest. Sebastian was awe struck that two species could find in each other a joint need that was simply about not feeling alone, not feeling like an outsider. He felt, on the one paw, that it was a shame both had to go outside their own species to get that level of acceptance, but on the other paw, he wouldn't exchange Celina for any dog he knew. He was already fond of her.

Over the following days and weeks, Celina would visit the garden after dark. The two perfected their art. Sebastian was so comfortable and solid, she felt really at ease sitting on him. He

38

was like a big brother. They had built their repertoire up to a good thunderous canter verging on a gallop by week three and it was clear they were meant to be.

Occasionally, instructions were misinterpreted and left became right or vice versa. The resulting fallop became something Celina was less and less ashamed of. If you never make a mistake, you'll never make anything worthwhile, her mother was fond of saying.

Raven and Millie discussed the changes they were seeing in their ally. Noses were a bit out of joint, with Raven in particular. He needed to give happiness to Sebastian, to feel he mattered to him. So, the feeling of him having fun all by himself was making Raven feel a bit whimpery.

- *Does anyone know why Sebastian is suddenly so confident in the garden at night?*
- *No actually…he used to be afraid of his own shite.*

- *Yeah, and he gets really lively too. Have you seen him belting around down there like an eejit? You'd swear he was being chased.*
- *I'd say he's just delighted with the coolness. Yeah, that's it, it's the coolness of the nighttime…*

The next night Celina and Sebastian were looking up at the stars and naming all the animals they would like to have been had they not been born a duck and a dog. They made each other laugh so hard with their choices. Sebastian said his number one choice would be a seahorse, he would love to know what it felt like to be light and floaty.

- *You do know that they don't feel light and floaty, don't you? They just feel like they always feel – they don't know it is light and floaty. It is just the feeling of normal to them, the same way your daily feeling is normal to you.*

Celina decided she would like to be a snake,

slithering over walls and through a lifetime, just slithering.

Suddenly, they saw a flash of light and arrested their talk in the hope that it was a shooting star. It came again but with the exact same intensity, that is when they knew they were dealing with something manmade.

- *Sebbie, what are you doing?*

Raven stiffly asked from a scared distance.

- (whispering) *Don't move, or do move, creep sideways with your wing elbows towards the wall. He is still some distance off – you have time.*

Sebastian instructed Celina.

- (quietly) *I'm already on it. See you tomorrow night and let's hope we're alone next time. Try to fix that will you?*

Raven moved closer in small increments, not really sure what he was looking at except for the outline of his dog lying on his back. So, Sebastian

41

did the side-to-side shuffle that implied he needed a good scratch.

Raven petted him on the head and joked with him. Sebastian had the closest soul bond with Raven and knew that if anyone was going to pick up on an oddity, it would be Raven. The love between them was pure and unconditional.

As they returned to the house together, the light from the moon grew dappled with intermittent cumulus clouds which interrupted the view. The distance carried with it the fragrance of yet another beautiful tomorrow. Before closing the door, Raven took one last look around the garden.

Tomorrow daytime would no doubt pass without a care, but it was the nighttime Sebastian began to fret about.

Practice Makes Perfect

It had to happen, she knew it, he knew it. He was a little bit peeved that the family went on the odd trip without him, so why shouldn't he take a trip of his own? The only thing standing in his way was the wall.

Sebastian had been sizing it up since about week two of Walla Walla practice. He had stretched his full length on it and his front paws could meet the arch at the top. If he could clutch the arch on the opposite side with his paws like a hook when he jumped, he would be able to balance there for a bit. He could then transfer the balance of weight forward with a surge of energy and jump to the bottom of the other side.

Since week two, he had been flexing his paw joints and individual toes for strength of purchase to secure success when he would find himself at that crucial balancing moment. He was also aware from watching Jackie tear bone dry carpet loads of moss off the wall when she was in one of her gardening vagaries, that some of the stones were loose. She had found herself sprawled out on the grass a couple of times when the loose stones gave her a helping hand in ridding themselves of the moss. He needed to be careful. He had to be ready for that and have the ability to transfer grip in an instant.

The forest would not be where Raven took him on walks, that was their own distinct place. It would be a much bigger wilder plane of endless trees, like a planet of trees: Sessile Oak, Beech, Scots Pine – breathlessly dense for all the breath they gave out. He could hear himself talking himself out of the wall jump. He decided to retreat upstairs to Raven's bedroom where he had been allowed to sleep since *that night*. Raven's bedroom door was always open now. No communication other than a double pat of the hand on his duvet was necessary. Sebastian needed some comfort, and Raven was the one to give it.

He would be back before they knew it, just like they would be back before he knew it as Millie would say imperiously when they took a trip and left him in charge of the house.

Celina called by the next night but decided to stay on the wall for a quick getaway. Sebastian was already in place.

- *Pst…*

    Pst…

- *I heard you the first time. I'm sizing it up. I won't be able to do it too often so don't be asking me to do a few practice runs. I'll get stuck on the other side with a busted paw, and then they'll have me indoors for the rest of the summer. Just give me a minute, I'm thinking.*

Celina backed off, she just prayed tonight

would be the night they would take their run through the Andaines Forest; confirming them as a lifelong Walla Walla. She intended to take him to *lot two* of the forest, not too big, not two small. She was keen to seal the deal. She never thought this moment would happen for her and she couldn't rest until it was official. Ducks usually lived to the age of ten and Berners could live that long too if they were lucky (big dogs die younger you see?) – both of them were five. They still had so much of a life together if their luck continued.

Sebastian decided to ignore the wall and then just focus on it last minute in some kind of  psychological move he had made up by himself. So, he ran around the garden building up a massive amount of velocity when he made the first move. His front knee knuckles let him know he was a little over a foot short of the top of the wall arch. He let out a muffled *humph* but rallied himself to try again. Around and around, again and again, sometimes riding wide of the jump altogether at the very last minute just to prove he could. Then it happened, he lined up, and cleared it with an impressively short amount of time spent in the balancing act at the top of the wall. Down…down…it didn't even result in a follop. He stood there standing, panting, ruffled, exhilarated, and ready to rock and roll.

So distracted with the feeling of pure freedom was he, that he forgot all about Celina. He started to walk forward with great purpose. She toddled, waddled, and shuffled after him trying to keep up, but his momentum was arresting, and he did not know where they were going; she did.

- *Sebastian, let me on.*

He waited a second to obey the command but was somewhere else entirely in his mind – he had never felt his eyes peeled so wide. Celina slid into position, and he wasn't too pleased that the first light pressure he felt was a command to go slowly. She explained that *lot two* of the forest was where their Walla Walla would take place and that they needed to conserve their energy to get there and still have what it took to complete the ritual. He fell in line; he'd heard of delayed gratification; he'd give it a go.

About an hour later the landscape began to change. Trees crossed their path more frequently, there was a uniformity in their bark, an army, a legion of thick territorial ownership. A sense of heavy enclosure enveloped him, he was under the reign and command of something he knew nothing about, and the ignorance was bliss; he could let go now. He felt a difference in her vibrations, she tried to mask it, but they were too united now for her to be able to fool him. He knew she just wanted to keep him calm, so he played along and pretended not to notice. They were getting close. His response to her commands became super sharp, he was entirely at her mercy. He thought of the Irish phrase *may the road rise to meet you* and he began to feel giddy, light-headed, and somewhat off balance.

The pressure began to increase, and his inner nervousness evaporated. He slid into a stupidly easily trot...polite canter...gallop...full on. Both laughed in doggery, then in duckery, then a mixture of both as their momentum gathered. When the hysterics were over, they tried every sound they could make, and the trees woke up to join in...throwing the musicality from branch to branch, and from truck to trunk for the lower keys. They hit a fork in the forest, but in true explorer style they chose the path less travelled on, falling into troughs of unevenness in this infrequently visited place, but recovering with ease to maintain their swiftness. Their mouths remained open by now, it sounded like a song, but no song either of them had ever heard before, now they provided the base, and the trees contributed the harmony, from leaf, to branch, to bark. There came a point where they didn't feel they were in control of what was happening to them anymore, a sort of spiritually assisted experience. Nothing seemed to need effort, wing and fur, beak and muzzle, they were each other or had been in another lifetime. The scent of her oiled skin was homely, and his steady musk brought her reassurance that she was meant to be here, that this experience was hers and his to claim. It had occurred with sublime ease; they were now a Walla Walla.

The pressure eased off and he respected her decision. The trees and the critters who occupied them knew their role had been validated and they returned to sleep. We are all just energy manifested as hard evidence of something. So whatever shape we arrive in, we can choose to be hard evidence of love, of kindness, of goodness, and only those who understand that, refuse to choose the opposite.

- *Mon petit étoiles.*

He nudged her playfully with his shoulder.

They lay under the stars in this forest of

equanimity, no answers were needed, no proofing was needed, no things were needed, they simply existed to enjoy – that was their only purpose.

The slow walk home was like a western mosey, side to side, hip to hip, click to click, beat to beat - the mission was accomplished, and they had the rest of their lives to appreciate the achievement of finding each other in what can sometimes feel like a lifetime of confusing and needless clutter.

As they approached the house, Sebastian could see over the wall that lights that were not usually on at this time of the night were on in the house. As they got closer, they could hear the family speaking in excited tones. Jackie was crying. Millie and Raven were not laughing at her as they usually did when she cried (and she cried often enough for an adult) – they always said she cried like a donkey. It started way down in a cavernous pit of somewhere indescribable and made its way up to an all-out bray, a comical hee-haw followed by a holler. And so, the pattern would repeat until she was finished. It was more than a little amusing

51

for them. But not this time.

He heard his name – lots of times. He thought he was in trouble, like the times Jackie got up to sit on the white seat during the night and kicked Sebastian on the head as she went there. Although Sebastian hadn't moved, the reason he got kicked in the head was apparently his own fault. He found what did and didn't get him into trouble quite confusing.

What to do this time? Celina advised lying low, to hop the wall now would mean lock up for Sebastian for the rest of the summer. Sebastian sure didn't fancy a telling-off, so he agreed, and they slept under the stars that night, not twenty meters from the house.

- *Can I ask you a question Celina?*
- *Sure.*
- *Why have you got a jumper on you?*
- *It was a gift.*
- *You must really like it.*

Celina found it hard to respond.

- *And you, you seem different, do you always live here Sebastian?*
- *Not all the time, no. I live in a place that looks like a teddy bear.*
- *Ireland.*
- *That's it.*

Trying to Make Things Better

Celina and Sebastian woke to the skull-shattering seven am church bells. To his amazement, Sebastian could hear that Raven and Sean were already up and having coffee and juice in the garden. They were discussing him:

- *I felt something.*
- *What?*
- *In the garden that night. There was something there when I came across Sebastian rubbing himself on the grass at the end of the garden.*
- *What was it?*

- *I said something, I don't know what, but there was a presence of some sort. That's what's happened, whatever that was, it is the reason Sebastian is gone. He would never leave us unless he had the company of something or someone else.*
- *It could be dog nappers, there's so much of that going about these days and they wouldn't realise he is neutered and useless for fathering puppies. Oh God help us. Where are you – SEBASTIAN? ...Come home you big eejit.*

Sean called out to the air in helpless awkwardness, loathing the sound of his own need. He looked greyer than usual and there were no sausages cooking this morning. Raven was fiddling with his hands in between fits and starts of conversation that seemed painful to partake in. Raven's voice was newly fragmented, it wasn't angry, it wasn't even irritated; it was wounded. He was a crab without its shell, as all adolescents were. What shell they develop will depend on their experiences and interactions in these precious years. Unfairness seemed much more obvious in his teens, *Mrs My Arse* was one thing, but this, this was something else. There would be hundreds more episodes to go but when you haven't got your armour fitted yet, weathering wounds can be excruciatingly raw.

On the other side of the wall, not twenty meters from the turmoil, Celina tried to figure out a way to fix what was turning into an unnecessary drama. She always understood she would have to co-love Sebastian, but the logistics of it were proving a bit finicky.

For now, she knew of a number of abandoned cottages and manors, either too rural or too expensive to renovate that would serve as shelter. None of them were more than five hectares away. They could retreat to one, in order to figure out how to remedy the situation so that everyone could be happy.

By threadbare, tumbledown, and tattered

house number three, Celina was losing her patience with Sebastian. He said he'd know it the minute he pushed the handle of the salon door down. An impressive tree-lined driveway would have been nice, but the warmth and peace of the salon was going to be everything. Celina couldn't understand why they didn't just stay in the first one they found, but he had a vision of that first walk through, and the flood of light that would greet him. It took them eight hours of trapsing around to find it. She reminded Sebbie that she was not an estate agent on commission, but he insisted the salon was a deal breaker for him. He had always wanted to play lord of the manor and now was his unique chance. Finding it was a welcome relief for Celina, who put no store by such things.

For Celina all the house needed to possess was a faint will to survive, and a tinchy burning ember at its heart. She could see how it would be fun to play house for now. Soon the family would receive Sebastian back, once she had thought up a believable solution that would not see him excessively minded for the remainder of the summer.

They would eat this evening and whittle down their options. In the meantime, Sebastian waltzed around the rooms and up and down the sweeping staircase like a true lord. He found the steps a little hard to negotiate with any grace, but he would stop now and again to look up at the ornate cornicing and romantic faded green and pink wallcovering in his new domain. Externally, he wandered proudly through what was the watercolour mark of a former formal garden. Signs of order were reimagined in his mind as he inspected the roses, he imagined them at pruning height when in fact they were towering over him.

He imagined his butler following him around asking if he could be of service.

- *No Geeves, all is in order…you may take the rest of the evening off.*

By day four Celina needed his opinion as she caught up with him on his daily strolls:

- *Who are you talking to?*
- *Myself, why?*
- *I was just wondering, have you ever had any of the following: leaves, seeds, nuts, fruits, tuber mushrooms, gum, or sap?*
- *I eat apples, pears, and white cherries when they fall off the trees in the garden, but I don't trust the furry things they call peaches – they feel too alive and skittish.*
- *Okay, okay…you are going to have to get creative with me here Sebastian on the food front. I found a lot of tree gum for this evening's tea; I hope you like it. I don't have the foraging skills of Jackie two legs. I don't know where she gets so much foodstuffs*

59

from and a casing to carry them in while she's at it. As I am not biologically a dog, I don't know what will satisfy you.

They bedded down for a number of nights to try to take stock of the situation.

Sebastian didn't know how to tell her without hurting her feelings, but when dogs get new food, their bodies tend to run it through them on the first instalment. So far, he had had a new type of food almost every single day and his bottom had been pretty busy. He had to pretend to be patrolling the grounds for intruders when Celina asked him why he was going outside so often. He wasn't used to getting caught short quite so often, and he was beginning to feel a little poorly.

The plan to return him wasn't going much better. Placing him prostrate on the front doorstep with a bunch of poisonous berries beside him was the best they had come up with so far. The hope was that the family would be so distracted by his ailment that they would forget he had jumped the wall in the first place. They had lost count of how many days they were there by the time Sebastian found it hard to take his daily walks.

Celina found an old bucket and filled it with water from a nearby stream, the least she could do was give him fresh water to keep him hydrated, she avoided the lakes and ponds. She might be used to the water in them, but he wouldn't be. He gulped the fresh water steadfastly on each fill. His teeth clashed off the sides of the bucket as he happily immersed his dehydrated gums, parched tongue, and grateful teeth inwards, down, deeper.

In the hope of finding a new food source, Celina flew further afield as the days wore on. One day she flew by Sebastian's maison secondaire. It was eerily quiet, though somebody was home. The back door was open and the makeshift plastic multicoloured back door fly screen was floating erratically like a crazed traffic policeman. Beside it, Celina noticed the shed door was ajar. That was where Sebastian's food was kept. She tried to think of how she could get it back to him. She had often watched as Raven filled his basin morning and night, religiously. She knew how much would get him up and moving again albeit with a few hours digestion time for it to take its effect. Perhaps there was a bucket with a handle in there that she could fill? Perhaps she could fly off with a small bucket of his regular food. She was nervous.

She landed on the shed roof, sizing up her options. The coast was clear. Deftly, she took the plunge and glided directly inside the shed. As she looked around for the food, she heard a colossal BOOM! The wind had closed the shed door tight. The internal buffering of the closure made it feel like she was underground. She stood there in stunned silence. It was coming towards the end of the summer. Celina wondered as she surveyed all that was in this ancient shed, how long it would be before someone would need to open the door again. They wouldn't be coming in for Sebastian's food any time soon, it was gone.

The sun came up and the sun went down, one time each. Nobody came. Why would they? If only they knew. All she could do was be ready. Finally, she heard footsteps, but they went away again. There could be nothing for it now, no time to lose, she would have to vocalise her doggery for the humans in the hope they would think it was Sebastian. She decided to do it straight away before the footsteps got too far away. She had to try to pretend to be Sebastian.

- *Waffle. Blaff.*

The footsteps halted. She knew she wouldn't be able to replicate his full-on bark, it was too deep. She decided instead to continue grumbling.

- *Nyaff...yaff.*

A few moments later she saw the shadow and felt the presence on the other side of the door. She was ready for them, whoever they were, she would show no mercy and fly right into their faces to get away – give them a few slaps around with her wings while she was at it, for good measure, because Sebastian would be home by now if he wasn't so afraid of the telling off he would get.

It worked and she broke free. From the dramatic *wooahs* and *feckin' hells*, Celina immediately knew she had just touched base with Jackie.

- *Lads, lads, there was a duck in the shed. Bloody hell. How did she get in there? What the hell, it felt weird.*
- *How do you know it was a 'she'?*

Predictably Raven pulled his mother up on gender assumptions but was soon distracted by a more immediate issue.

- *It was on the wall previously, I'm sure of it. What would she want with the shed?* Jackie wondered.
- *I wonder was that it?*
- *You wonder was that what?*
- *The presence, the something I felt in the garden that night.*
- *Sebastian has run off with a duck? Jeepers! I thought I was out of ideas.*

As Celina flew off empty-beaked, she was dumbfounded that the family had either moved Sebastian's food or given it away. This particular forage was meant to be a great surprise for him; now she had nothing.

When she returned to their abandoned manor house, she called out to him. He had taken to sleeping in the main salon as the cross draft in its various parts and the dual aspect of its long French windows supplied him with a calming sense of peace.

Sebastian's return was becoming less and less likely. Though the days were *très chaud*, the nights were beginning to point towards the wild, irrational nature of early autumn and the fruits began to introduce themselves to the ground. Fruit fall after fruit fall had not been picked up for many decades at Sebastian and Celina's new abode, and it gave the soil a strangely scorched appearance not unlike the ambers and tangerines of autumn itself or the bile of Sebastian's stomach which was beginning to make a frequent and unwelcome appearance in recent days.

Help

Raven

A frantic shit show at this stage…

Arson

Why don't you put posters of him up and around the place?

Raven

Good idea, I'll do that, how to get them printed? Handmake them?

Arson

Write it out in French, use google translator – photocopy them in that local large town, the one with Super U in it.

Raven

I've heard that when you put in content to translator, it might not come out the other side meaning the same thing.

Arson

Offer a reward then, that'll be clear.

Raven

The French aren't motivated by money...numpty!

Arson

Keep it lemon!

Raven kept up the bravado with his friends at home, as though he was taking the whole thing in his stride.

- *Jackie, why don't you put it on Facebook?* Sean said.
- *Great yeah: 'Dog missing, last seen in the Loire France, PM me if you see him around the Cliffs of Moher.'*
- *I'm only trying to help.*
- *I know you are love, sorry, it all feels so hopeless. The longer it goes on the further away he could be.*

Jackie and Sean held hands tightly as they took all the various trails they could find through the Andaines Forest within a reasonable distance of home. Their legs ached; their hearts were miserable. Millie was readying herself for the media interview and all that they would need to say in it – she had settled on dog nappers. It would have to get some local media attention surely. She made a great pot of tea, just the right strength and kept the family in scones, jam, *le pain*, & ham. She kept the house clean and did the ironing and washing. She was Millie, and she found her way to be useful. They were ever so grateful for her.

Night after night, phone calls and messaging home for support and advice ended in the family retreating dismally to their rooms, wracked with the agony of not knowing. The mornings were filled with cloying attempts to come up with new ideas as to where he could be. Each of them had grown closer to one another, united in their common grief. Celina couldn't help but stop by to observe them from a nearby empty pigeon house; she was wracked with the agony of knowing.

One day she went by, and the car was gone, the shutters were down. It did not look good. Her heart fluttered, trembled, scrambled. She made her way around to the back and saw that the garden furniture had been put away and the house showed no signs of life. One shutter was not fully closed. Sitting inside the kitchen eating bread and ham was Sean, alone. She resolved not to tell

Sebastian, he was delicate enough as it was.

The following morning it was raining, the kind of rain that seemed to dance its enthusiasm on her like an overexcited child, each drop demanding to know where Celina was going. Sebastian's digestion had settled down, he was keeping hydrated, and he was able to manage the odd morsel of food that she could find, but she was still desperate to find the good stuff he was used to.

She was determined that she would find a way to get Sean to find Sebbie, for she had resolved to call him by that familiar nickname as a gesture towards Raven, who must now, be a different boy altogether.

She watched Sean come and go, she saw him pick up his baguette at the Mairie's office each morning and converse with the locals in his pidgin French, then retreat to the house where he remained until evening. After six, he would go for a walk to the secret forest Raven and Sebastian used to go to. Up until now it was a case of *ces't interdite* for anyone but Raven and Sebastian. Raven had clearly shared its location since Sebastian's disappearance. This evening Celina followed Sean. As she reached the stream Raven and Sebastian used to sit at together, it had become obvious where the food from the shed had gone. Raven had created a breadcrumb trail of it all the way from the house to the forbidden forest stream.

She picked up four pieces of it and flew back to Sebastian. At first, he sniffed at them as though they were yet another new thing to try. Bit by bit his memory returned, and he ate them as his heart broke into pieces.

Outside in the family garden Celina regularly observed Sean talking to Jackie, Raven and Millie through what I have come to know as a mobile phone. He seemed happier when this happened, though he was a little concerned that his medicines had not arrived in the latest postal delivery, and he was running short. He felt that he too would need to give up and go home soon, the hospital needed to see him.

Every day from there on in, she brought Sebbie more pieces of food, he was returning, if only in little glimpses. She knew she was depleting the trial to his home, but the trail could not be followed from where they were anyway. She became more and more adept at carrying his food pieces and managed to cram a few more pieces into her cheeks whenever she could.

One day she was looking in the kitchen window, she wanted to quietly observe Sean to see if some idea might dawn on her over how to get the two of them back together, Sean on his own was perhaps safer and easier than trying to return Sebastian to the whole family. Just then, she felt something grab her from behind.

-   *There you are you little feckwit.*

It was Sean.

-   *Wait until Raven hears what I've just found. What on earth are you wearing?*

The scramble was ugly, at one stage she was

under Sean's armpit, and he wasn't keeping up with his showers since the family had left that was for sure. He seemed truly disgusted and distracted over Celina's jumper. She got free and flew over the garden wall and made straight for their house. Celina was about two miles short of the house when Sebastian grew alert. He could smell the family; he could smell the aroma of his family in the air. He began to walk, feebly at first, in the direction of the scent only to find it was getting stronger and stronger the closer and closer Celina got.

- *It's time I went home now Celina. I'll face whatever happens. How come you smell of them?*
- *Sebbie, a lot has happened since you were last home.*
- *It doesn't matter. Lead the way, you know where they are.*
- *No.*
- *What?*

73

- *No. You'll never be allowed to see me again. This will be the end if you go.*
- *I'm going and that's final. I will see you on the wall later, hold on, maybe leave it a week and we can still Walla Walla in my back garden, okay?*
- *I'm not letting you go.*
- *Goodbye Celina. À bientôt.*

Sebastian realised that without Celina who was carrying the family scent, he could not direct himself. So far that wasn't a problem because she was coming with him anyway. Inadvertently, he allowed her to keep pace. She didn't realise that in her frantic protestations, she was leading him home. They walked along saying nothing to each other with big broad heavy purposeful footsteps. Within two miles of home, he got it again, the scent faintly on the air and this time it wasn't coming from Celina. He began to pick up the pace and to his amazement, he could take it up to a gently paced run. Celina began to panic. She flew above him attempting to thwart his progress. He gathered momentum as she tried to keep up. Just then her jumper had snagged on a fallen snarly, gnarly piece of tree bark that had cracked at a blunt angle. The bark seemed intent on doing damage to anything that tried to cross it, she did, and she was snared.

Her jumper began to unravel. Thread by thread. Her jumper wasn't the only thing that was unravelling, so too was her sense of control over Sebastian. She had to fly and halt him or save her jumper. She tried both. Her beak was attempting to yank the thread free. One uncovered wing wouldn't be too bad: maybe. As one wing was freed it created the problem that both wings were now imbalanced, and she was losing her direction. The heavier one was making her go around in circles above Sebastian's head. She tried to hold the thread at a point beyond which it could not unravel. She tried to snap it free of the snag, but her beak just wasn't cut out for it. She screeched at Sebastian for help.

- *Why doesn't everybody leave me alone? Everyone wants something from me. I just want a sausage and some peace and quiet. I'm going home.*

The snag was finished with Celina's right wing and was making moves on her main body. She lost her grip on the thread and started swirling around and around and around like a ball of wool being fired across a room. Dizzy and woozy - she straightened up to see her whole body free of wool save for the left wing – then that too slid off like a satin sleeve. Now she could keep pace with him, but she was constantly looking at herself. She was amazed at the beauty of her feathers and the curves of her body.

This would be an easy win now. She steadied herself above Sebastian's real collar. You see, he had two collars, one real one and one for walks that would tighten a little if he got too frisky and tried to drag a person along with overexcitement.

She was about to slide her webbed feet under his real collar and use her new powerful wool-free wings to bring him to a stop. Something stopped her. Freedom. She was free for the first time since her early childhood. The air was blowing through her wings easily, refreshingly. For every wing flap she was achieving twice the result. She let him go; she was unravelled in every way possible.

Celina gave up completely, allowing Sebastian to complete the remaining journey by himself. It felt somewhat hopeless, at his worst, he was going around and around in circles, but he'd get there eventually. She couldn't bear to watch him find the Hegarty house vacant. But she created the problem, and it was up to her now to fix it.

Sebastian never looked back, his big mutton head down low - intent on one thing only, being surrounded by that scent of home.

How to Get Knitted

The Dolmen de Bagneux, south of Saumur, was part of the backdrop of Celina's upbringing. It is twenty-three meters long and is built from fifteen large slabs of the local stone, weighing over five hundred tons. It is the largest in France and provides immeasurable protection from inclement weather for the local ducks who nestle into the natural troughs that surround them. People presume that ducks like the rain.

Equally impressive is a favourite old haunt of

Celina's, the Château de Saumur. The grounds of this castle had been home to Celina's ancestors since the 10th century. The chateau has changed human hands several times, but the one constant was the spritely presence of the Muscovy ducks.

 You see the sun goes up and the sun goes down on the human world, but that is of little interest to wildlife – people come; people go.

This beautiful habitat, just another wonderous setting to life in France, was where Celina experienced the world as a small duckling, just like many a lucky duck before her. The sheen of her charcoal feathered wings and that of her family's white feathers had taken on a smidgen of the hue of the local Tuffeau stone over the years. Their red splashed birthmarked faces and thickset necks had become a totally necessary part of the environmental imagery of Saumur. On most scorching summer days, the ducks were to be found gathered under The Cessart Bridge with its cool walls. They treasured the experience of lounging around the low-level lapping of the Loire.

Back when the town was a national soldierly equestrian centre, images of Celina's ancestors became the black, white, and red emblem of the national military cavalry school.

Like most large towns, Saumur had its fair share of 'bored' teenagers, however the teens of Saumur never let that boredom spill over into mischief where the Muscovy ducks were concerned, they had a protective admiration for their feathered friends. This admiration was bred into them from a very young age by responsible parents. The greatest shame for any Saumur parent was to be told their child had in any way thwarted a Muscovy duck – and no wildlife has suffered because of it.

In fact, so intertwined with each other are Saumur teenagers and the Muscovy duck, that during the Battle of Saumur in World War II, teenage cadets of the cavalry school with a little help from the Muscovy, fought off enemy invasion together. The Muscovy red splashed faces were less familiar to foreigners, so the ducks came up with a plan. They decided to feign acute rabid infection. The teen cadets pretended to be 'unclean' as a result of contamination, they feigned belly ache and delirium on a scale that halted the enemy in their tracks. They even waved the enemy off with their red cavalry neck scarves to declare the area infectious. The plan worked better than any manmade machinery of war. Few people knew in those days which diseases were catching and which diseases were harmless, so they were afraid of them all. The ducks behaved erratically, drooling, snapping at thin air, and giving the impression of being feral and highly dangerous. They were an eco-friendly deterrent that worked a treat. The enemy steered clear of

81

what they couldn't control.

Celina was told this story often by her proud mother. Celina herself was a petite but stout duckling for her breed, she had four brothers and two sisters of standard size and shape. Her mother had a broken wing. The wing trailed along the ground and was a cumbersome addition to motherhood, but she managed. Celina, like her mother, would also in time become adept at managing life with added burdens.

In every other way Celina was a stereotypical Muscovy, she had a torpedo shaped body, rounded head, and a slightly flattened and rounded bill. Her family type was prone to growing up to nine pounds in weight, an average Celina had broken by the age of two. Waterfowl have incredibly cohesive and attractive colours, and this is where Celina was not just stereotypical but exemplary. Her plumage with its heightened colour splash and fabulous lustre caused her a combination of pride and embarrassment. The females of her paddling would admire Celina for hours on end saying how it was a freak of nature for one bird to be blessed with such a saturation of sheen and shade. Her bulbous crest was heartened by the approval, she was glad of it. Everybody deserves to feel unashamedly proud of at least one unique thing nature has given them.

An added loveliness she possessed, is that she was a country duck, and therefore had a softer voice. In the countryside the ducks have less noise to compete with than their urban counterparts. Formation flying was practiced in two seasons of the year (as a matter of habit) to keep up their wind resistance – but the Muscovy chose never to leave their beloved Saumur. They acquired most of their food in and around France's largest river, and the options were plentiful.

Celina's mother was Marie Claire. She was a pragmatic lady who wanted her ducklings to be proud of all their efforts in life and to make do with what the universe had given them. In the evening when her work was done, she would gather her chicks around her, and they would

watch the world go by. Though she never said anything, Celina picked up on her mother's sorrow at not being able to fly. She watched as her cousins; mallards and white heads, and her distant relatives; starlings - and even low flying pheasants took to the air to some degree. It would be different if Maire Claire had never flown, but she knew what it was like to fly, and that made her broken wing all the sadder. Her reliance on relatives to teach her children to fly in their early years was a sobbing, whimpering catastrophe for her. The day she saved Celina's brother from a pasting on the road had cost her, but who wouldn't pay for their child's near-fatal decision with a broken limb?

She never wanted a fate like hers to befall her chicks, so she began to knit with great purpose. Marie Claire knew where to get the wool and knew only to take a ball at a time in order not to get caught. All Celina's siblings were too fast for her and flew the nest before she got a chance to fit them with an anti-wing breaker – her own unique invention. Celina knew how much it meant to her and although she didn't want it either, she let her do it, it was important to Maire Claire. It made her happy that she had guaranteed, one of her chicks would never have a broken wing. The problem was, she didn't stop at the wings - she continued to knit until Celina was in an entire casing of wool. Her perfect plumage was now hidden for life, and all to protect against the off chance of an accident that may never happen.

The enduring bond between mother and daughter weathered the problems of Celina having to go through the remainder of her life wearing a jumper. It weathered the distraught whisperings of her relatives, it weathered all with an enduring nightly kiss of reassurance from her mother that this was the best way to guarantee safety for her. Being protective was a cornerstone of the Muscovy way of doing things.

Celina refused to leave her mother's side. For a

long time, it was just the two of them. She continued to live in seclusion even after her mother's death. Her mother had used the same nest every year, it was skilfully inaccessible but dappled with sunlight through the cracked arches of the Cessart Bridge. It was there as Celina grew a little older and wiser, that she hatched the idea of becoming mistress of her own destiny, jumper, or no jumper.

She foraged for food in the grass, collected twigs to improve the nest, but none of it quite felt the same as it had when her mother was alive. The nest became just a physical assembly of well woven twigs, its sense of home was gone – it had left with her mother. She didn't even possess the joy of preening her feathers since her mother had encased her in love. Bit by bit, Saumur did not feel like somewhere she belonged anymore. As the gaggle of sentries kept watch over the whole cohort, she saw them throw a kindly reassuring glance up at her now and again. But she felt like she drained the group's energy. She made tentative plans to leave, to see if she could reinvent herself somewhere where nobody knew she ever looked any different to the way she does now.

Healthy ducks often look out for their injured comrades, but as Celina was both psychologically and physically fit – they really didn't know what to do to help. One night the air was paper thin. The stillness was full of promise. Celina approached the gaggle members who had just come on collective duty. Every footstep she made sounded soggy and sad. She did not need to speak, all the ducks who were old enough had already made their union with a dog and they knew what Celina pinned for. A potential adventure away from home was going to be Celina's last chance to fulfill her birthright. They instinctively knew she was going to do something brave, and they were rooting for her.

Though she would not be an adept flier or have stars to navigate any kind of familiarity - she was ready to go. They knew it, and they fussed around her honking their encouragement.

People don't understand that all waterfowl can feel pain and can feel emotions just like humans. People don't understand a lot of things.

Cherbourg

In the aftermath of their unpleasant parting, Celina could not have felt more sorry for what she had done, she was sorry for all of it. When we are afraid, we can do terrible things. Most bad behaviour comes from fear. She needed to operate now from the goodness she knew was inside her. Creating her birthright of a Walla Walla with Sebastian was never meant to hurt anyone, least of all him. She'd been selfless all her life up until this and her heart now ached for the Hegartys. She needed to fight the last of any inherited fear she had and find Cherbourg.

With the last of the food trail pieces she could find; she dropped a sparse trail for Sebastian to follow her to the *Route de Mortain,* she spelled the trail out in the letters *C-H-E-R-B-O-U-R-G* in the hope that he would recognise the name. In due course he arrived complainingly, no doggery or duckery was spoken, things were still too raw. He knew she was sorry, and that she hadn't intended for things to turn out the way they did. But more importantly after witnessing the shutters pulled down so completely on the house, he knew what Cherbourg meant.

* * *

It was a lovely damp evening with a chorus of varied birdsong to see them off. They took the *Route de Mortain,* a greenway which was wide and clear, it invited them forward, congratulating them on a sensible decision. The evening held all the promise of mid-April, despite the reality that they could feel the terse tap of October on their shoulders. The talk in the trees was full of excitement, they were in for a good ruffling. Celina and Sebastian's journey seemed in tune with what nature wanted.

Celina had heard of Cherbourg of course, over the years, but she had never gone that far north in France before. They would take all of the greenways on offer between The Loire and St Malo and there were many – besides the odd hop, skip and jump across a secondary road – the route could be completed almost exclusively off the beaten track which is just what they needed. After that would come the hard part, they would have to take their chances from St. Malo over to Cherbourg on main roads. Choosing the cover of night Celina felt would be the best way to negotiate this final leg of their journey. It felt good to be so decisive and getting on with things one way or the other.

The greenways were mainly hidden under branch cover and so were damper and less exposed to the departing summer sunshine. They fell in unison with each other's step. Her feet were all squelchy welchy in the damper sections of their path, and sometimes the webbing would be so sunken and suctioned under with mud that the claw parts had a negligible amount of say in what happened with her next move. She found it super frustrating but felt she deserved it. Was it punishment for taking Sebastian all to herself when he was never hers exclusively? Her feet felt ridiculously impractical for the job, in short, she felt like a great lolloping dolloping ugly duck.

Sebastian dearly wanted to be reunited with his family. He would do anything to get 'home', they were his home. He couldn't even scent them on the air anymore. He had three default emotional settings, content, super content or not happy. Right now, and for a long time hence he was not happy. Celina had a mammoth task ahead of her, but she was determined to get him home to Ireland.

He was grateful Celina was trying to help him, but there were times he felt he might have been better off on his own. He thought there were times when she was getting stuck in the mud on purpose. She was trying his patience, and in his unkinder moments he thought she was seriously trying to scupper the whole plan. She may have been subconsciously delaying having to say goodbye to him forever, but when he thought about it logically, it could not have been intentional. The whole plan to get him home was hers in the first place. Sebastian wouldn't have had a clue how to organise this. Celina loved him, and in doing so she knew she would have to let him go at the end of this expedition. He felt bad for thinking poorly of her, especially when she would have to return the hundreds of kilometres back, all on her own.

He was living now off his own muscle and sinew, there was a raw edginess in it that he quite enjoyed.

His departure, if it happened, would return her to a state of aloneness – they both knew it, they both quietly accepted it. But a Walla Walla was never meant to be separated. So how had this happened?

On the first evening of their journey, they reckoned they had covered about thirty kilometres, without agreement, they both naturally slowed down to a stroll, each knowing they were done for the day. They could feel the vibration of human activity and had gotten used to the different energy from a nearby hamlet, a nearby village, or a full-on town without physically seeing them. Each with its own soul spoke differently, the bigger the town the colder its energy. The chances of food however were higher the colder the energy got.

Celina sat down and attempted to clean her feet. As a duck, her feet were her pride and joy, along with her feathers, she felt ashamed over the state they were in. Sebastian, though bedraggled, was charged with the energy of a dog on a mission. He went into town under cover, using the passing lights of cars as his cue to move forward. Bravery entered his soul, he knocked over bins, ripped open packets and ate everything he found. He would need to take the pressure off Celina tonight, she was the one who knew where they were going but she was vulnerable too at times. One more half-eaten *pain au chocolat* and he would have enough strength to start looking for food for her.

He found an unopened jar of something called pate that had a fat and happy duck on the front of it who was licking his or her bill. She won't believe her luck when she sees this, he thought. He took it as gently as he could and balanced it between his teeth. Off he trotted, stooping demurely to hide his eyes and white chest from oncoming lights.

When he put the jar in front of her, he was puzzled at her expression. She looked horrified. She explained to him that the contents of the jar contained the liver of a duck that had been force-fed in what amounted to a torture chamber where some ducks are trapped. In these torture chambers, when their liver is extended enough, they are killed, and their liver is mashed up and put into these jars.

- *Is this some kind of sick joke?* she barked.

Sebastian instantly forgave himself because he could, only if he intended to hurt her should he feel bad. So off he went again in search of something else for her, but not before digging a great big hole and putting the jar into it. He then filled in the hole lickedy split and tried to remember the thing his family did with their short legs when they would see a dead animal at the side of the road, he thought it went 'God bless your little life?' He lifted his right paw and swung it about his head and shoulders a bit, content in the knowledge, that it was something similar to this. He would have to be silent for a little bit, and then everything could return to normal. Yes, that's how it went.

Sebbie went the more natural route this time. He overturned rocks and decayed fallen wood. He rummaged and foraged for all the insects and grubs and worms he could find. He wondered if this was where the French dinner of a thousand servings of something small came from. His mouth was so big that occasionally he would accidentally swallow the fly he was intent on delivering to Celina. Eventually, Celina nodded her head from side to side as if to say '*enough*', Sebbie was relieved but proud, it was a delicate job well done.

The sun rose lightly next morning, it was like a butterfly – they would be light-footed today, the adjacent river was running downstream. All was well. The universe was on their side.

They decided they were the Lion and Dorothy from the Wizard of Oz today, they played foot games and *skipped to My Lou* and because they were falling around laughing, they had unbeknownst to themselves covered fifty kilometres this second day. They celebrated the halfway milestone with a hug and a kiss, and they were amazed at how well they felt. It would be a night of sugar, berries, currants, and the odd midget thrown in for good measure. Sebbie took it easy as he didn't want to get the runs. With little enough weight on as it is, he could ill afford to lose so much as a quarter of a pound. He drank plenty of water in the nearby river and ate grass to give his stomach a good clear out. Lamb and rice, his favourite dinner could soon be a reality that he would taste again. He savoured that thought.

By day three, a new determination set in for

both. Their heads went down, little was said between them. The back needed to be broken on this journey and today would be the day, there was to be no messing, strides would have to be serious. At the end of the day, they would be over the hill and genuinely able to get excited about the potential of seeing an Irish ship.

So, what was left by day four was the last fifty kilometres to the coast and then the treacherous last leg of the journey when they would need to work double time to negotiate the open roads. They hoped they wouldn't get picked up by human well-wishers. They had a job to do, and the last thing they wanted was humans offering them bed and breakfast and intercepting the whole mission.

They barely spoke on the live and busy roads to Cherbourg. They ran, they ducked (if you'll pardon the pun) and they coughed the fumes of the human world vehemently from their purified chests. All they could feel from each other was a silent sense of watchfulness. Both understood the imperative of *the less said the better* during this phase. What to avoid and what to embrace was quietly known. This was an operation for eyes, ears, and furtive dexterous movements.

For some strange reason Sebbie thought the sight of anything Irish was going to be met with a great big fanfare, a delight like no other. The port itself was a tremendous anti-climax. The sight of the colour green with a shamrock on a chimney stack of the boat was however a scintillating relief, he could feel a tension leave his body that he didn't even know was there – it had lived inside him for so long.

Celina's excessive chatter and instructions over who to approach and how were nothing but a background noise now, an underwater globule of mush. Ireland was a boat ride away.

The gendarmerie were standing around arguing over a rugby match where it was clear they believed France had been done out of a win. From the scant activity evident, no boats were departing soon, so time was on their side. No problem Sebbie thought, he had waited God knows how long so far, three or so days was not going to faze him.

A last-minute wobbler halted him in his tracks. What would he say to Celina now? What if he is put on the wrong boat? What if he is sent to a rescue centre? What if?

Celina grabbed him by the shoulders and told him it was time to be brokeny brave. That means brave even though it might seem silly to be so.

- *You're loved Sebbie. I love you. They love you.*

He winded himself with the lump that appeared in his throat, he didn't want to leave her, but he really had to go.

- *Why don't you perch on the boat and follow me?*
- *Because it's not for me Sebbie. The boat is for you, for your family.*

She pushed him forward and waddled off as fast as she could.

One of the gendarmeries was distracted by the sight of this four-legged creature making its way towards them. He slapped his colleague on the  arm who was in full flight over the rugby match. They were trying to make out what it was, a dog was their nervous guess, but what on earth had happened to it? There were chunks of hair missing, it was so unsteady and emaciated it looked like it was asking them to observe the very last few steps it would ever take.

The first gendarmerie who noticed Sebbie, got down on his hunkers. Sebbie knew this trick, it meant kindness. He mosied over.

A second gendarmerie began to Google black, white, brown, large and they were shocked to see that what they were looking at was the remanence of a Bernese Mountain Dog. A third gendarmerie went away all the while looking at his phone. He quickened his pace as he entered a small grey box with a window and a single door. It looked like a pretend building. At this stage a port official had joined the gendarmerie and he offered Sebastian something to eat, which he had had in his pocket. Sebastian turned his head the other way. A minute or two later the third gendarmerie came out of the grey box with a lady who was wearing what looked like a set of blue pyjamas. She had a circular machine in her hand and as she approached Sebastian, she switched it on.

At this stage some other members of the port staff had gathered around Sebastian and when the lady in the blue pyjamas ran the circular machine over Sebastian's left shoulder, something happened, a noise, slight and almost imperceptible. After that, everything went quiet as the lady started hitting her phone with her finger, a lot. It seemed like forever, but everyone waited patiently. Acknowledgement, relief, pets galore for Sebastian ensued. One of the port officials joked that his family was had, that he was the runt of the litter at best, and more probably a crossbreed of some sort. They had no idea of his former glory. Suddenly his status had risen to new heights, the air was full of potential. The lady returned to her grey box and came back with a lead, and a muzzle. The gendarmerie went back to their conversations in an animated way and Sebbie disappeared into the grey box. There was only one way out of that grey box and that was the way in, so Celina waited patiently between two parked-up container lorries. She had a perfect vantage point behind the first and second wheel of the right side of a truck advertising *Conor Murphy International Freight.*

It was five days before Celina caught a glimpse of Sebastian again. He seemed sturdier on his legs, and he was handed over to staff wearing the words Brittany Ferries on their clothes. He was handed over by the lady who was (*by the way*) still wearing her pyjamas. The ferry staff fussed and *fouthered* over him and he politely asked them to get on with the job of getting him on the boat. Of course, he didn't actually say that to anybody, but Celina understood his energy. She guessed he knew she was still there, somewhere abouts.

They walked towards the ship which was now full of animated activity. Cars, vans, dogs, campervans, horses, caravans, lorries, everyone in the world now suddenly seemed to be going to Ireland. Sebbie disappeared into a large glass tunnel and walked through it towards the ship. The last she saw of him was the white tip of his big sorry-looking black and brown tail, it was raised in blissful surrender, he was content. He knew she was watching him, but he couldn't afford to look back.

The great thing about Cherbourg is that it is used almost exclusively for travel to Ireland and so Celina knew she had done her part to get Sebastian home. She had heard that Ireland was small in comparison to France. This made her even more sure that what she had done was the right thing – the smaller the place, the easier it would be to find Sebastian's family. On the other hand, his landing in Ireland and what would happen to him at that stage, would be out of her little webbed feet. Celina had heard nothing but glowing reports about the Irish as a race. They were said to be kind, caring, generous and quite the goodest of people.

When she guided him to the port, she explained to him that she would have to leave him in the hands of the port gendarmerie, he didn't seem to understand or care. Her plan worked; the gendarmerie came through for her very unique Walla Walla.

In her mind's eye she hopped his back one last time and stroked her feet against the back of his ears. She directed him forward, further.

- *Go n-éirí an bóthar leat,* Celina whispered into the salty air.

He roused in her imagination, and in reality, to the sound of his native Irish language coming through the bars of his double kennel. He had caught her soft breath on the inky oceanic night. It was here he would safely bed down for the eighteen-hour crossing to his homeland. People don't think ducks feel emotions, people don't think. A small part of her wanted to change her mind and perch on the boat bound for Ireland, but she didn't have one ounce of courage left.

He was leaving, on the next ship to Ireland – she couldn't bear to watch it. His sorry frame, emaciated in comparison to the one she once galloped on through the Andaines Forest, had now finally disappeared beyond view. She was hopeful for him but was beside herself with sadness that she would probably never see him again. Au revoir my *Anamchara.* Au revoir my friend.

 Celina slept in a rocky alcove on St Malo beach that night, the youthful brash waves and nasty cold felt like the last piece of turbulence she would have to endure in this strange life lesson, she accepted it graciously. The following day she decided she needed to see Saumur again. She needed the sights,

sounds and smells of the familiar. Alone, she plodded the long journey home, her heart an empty chasm, an echo chamber of loss.

Alone Again

And so it was that, like it or not, Celina was again without company. It brought some welcome changes and some unwelcome changes.

She wallowed and swallowed (though it was hard), and she slugged and trudged all the way back, so clearly on her own, like a beacon of aloneness. Her feet were at it again, squelching and welshing.

Having spent so long on her own in the general scheme of things, she tried to recollect herself and rally. Celina had one saving grace at this point in our story, her thunderous ability to be alone without a completely and utterly broken spirit. It was an annoying quality to some. Emily Dickinson once said that:

> *'Hope' is the thing with feathers -*
> *That perches in the soul -*
> *And sings the tune without the words -*
> *And never stops - at all -*

Hope, no matter how frozen and beaten, wouldn't need much encouragement to come back and sing that slightly annoying song. She'd try to find words for the lyric-free song. She'd done it before, and she'd do it again.

- *No, no regrets...*

Nobody could hear her. Celina turned up the volume...and changed the song.

- *Chanson d'amour, rat a tat a tat. Each time I hear, rat a tat a tat, chanson, chanson, d'amour...*

She laughed and chuckled with herself and wound it down at her own pace and in her own time. That was a nice thing about having fun by herself, she didn't need to put up with anyone else's version of when it was time to stop or go.

She had to focus on the positives, someone clever once said, 'It is better to have loved and lost than never to have loved at all.' She agreed with this sentiment. It was over, but the main thing is – it had happened, and she never thought it would. She started to look at all the things she never thought would happen, the Walla Walla was just one. She was declared not to have a snowflake's chance in hell of surviving life at all with her big woolly jumper on, and that turned out to be untrue. She was now five years old and had no reason to believe she wouldn't live just as long as any other Muscovy, particularly now that she had shed her jumper and had become more physically active.

She had been to St. Malo on foot! Not a lot of ducks from Saumur could claim that. There is a tiny win in everything. Sebbie loved her, and he had given his love freely. She didn't love herself right now, but she had a great penchant for fun and that was a start towards feeling less broken.

Saumur was her destination this time, back to

where her life began and where she decided she would return. She was who she was, there were worse out there. She once left the place feeling ashamed and unlovable. That was also untrue. Sebbie loved her, the love may be cracked, dishevelled and on its way to another country but, *ces't la vie*. She'd had love and that is what counted.

It's a cliché of course but Saumur really did look smaller on her return. When you are reared in one place, its scale becomes about more than measurements. Now it was back to measurements for her, she was bigger than the feelings she'd had in Saumur. Life was bigger than those feelings. Perspective creates scale.

The Summer had parched the earth, and the soil around the Loire's water was rock hard, despite the depths, volume, and luminosity of what was just a stone's throw from her feet. It was going to take a while for all that fresh new water to penetrate the banks.

She looked at her old home and decided to peruse the town. She toddled down streets and laneways she thought the Muscovy were less welcome on, it didn't feel that way now.

She could not afford to think of Sebastian right now. It tormented her. She had no control over what was happening to him. She now needed to take care of herself and take care of herself she would.

Celina took a fancy to a fishing pont on the Loire which was somewhat used. She felt if she hung around here long enough, she would get the cast-offs from unwanted bate hooks, why make life hard on yourself?

The rear of the pont was shored up with sand and gravel, perfect for her dryer moments. She was less afraid of humans than her local counterparts, she had seen them in action and although they could be a mighty nuisance, they were also mesmerizingly clever. So, she would hedge her bets and go fifty/fifty on a relationship with them. They could admire her close-up and take photos, even selfies, to beat the band, and she would get free food. It was a *win win*. At night when the fishermen (and it was usually men) had gone home, she took to the task of carving her name into the deck of the pont. She had become quite the celebrity with her plumage out on show, how it was so fresh and pristinely kept was the subject of much speculation. However, she loved her name and didn't want to wait until one of the humans decided to name her themselves. She made the carving discrete so that they would think the whole thing was their idea, two and two and all that! One thing you could be sure of was an egotistical streak in humans and thank God for it or they would have made little progress, like the kind of progress that enabled Sebbie to get back to Ireland. Somebody thought a leap from France to Ireland could happen for a regular dog; and so, it did. The carved Celina eventually became *Celina and Sebbie* with a love heart shape. She knew they would name her Celina, but they would spend some time wondering about Sebbie, just like she would – for the rest of her life.

And so, before she knew it seasons had passed.

Wounds had healed and hearts had mended, just mended mind you not gotten restored completely. And that is how she knew life could move forward, with the cracks and the crevices, with the weight and the gain and the loss.

Celina had left her own land and hooked up with an exotic style Walla Walla, this became accepted by most of the local dogs and ducks. She earned the respect that being brave brings. Those who try things become sounding grounds for those who don't, and rather than get annoyed with them for their lack of grit, she felt instead great empathy for those who don't leave, for those who don't change. In fact, she felt some degree of envy it must be said, what must it be like to never take a chance on an unknown outcome? Or more importantly, to never want to take a chance? How amazing might it be to be just content exactly as you are?

The worms were plentiful both through hook bait and deep foraging just above the waterline where aquatic plants were readily available as a side dish. However, as her fame increased, humans brought her some new delicacies like scrambled eggs, sliced grapes and refined dry grain, the origin of which she knew not, they were delicious. All was well.

The beginning of autumn was showing its vinegary glimmer; the harvest was fine, and food and sustenance were hers in exchange for satisfying the curiosity of humans—a fair deal for both parties.

Home is a Feeling

The routine of her life in Saumur continued rhythmically and she made a clear resolve not to see it as her former home but as her home anew. Her mother made her decisions previously and Celina would now make hers. She remembered her mother fondly, no judgements, no regrets, just affection.

The Saumur sunset which often walked out of the day backwards was the most romantic in all of France, it was kind, warm, and horribly sorry for any anger expressed during the midday. It seemed to acknowledge Celina as royalty as it bowed out. She felt so at peace here.

She was nodded at reverently by mothers each

morning, mothers with their squadron of chicks would tell their young that Celina conducted her Walla Walla with a foreign dog who did a runner on her. He was a beast of unknown origin, Sebbie, was possibly his name (though they had no confirmation of this). This foreign dog grew to be a legend with time and storytelling:

- *No, he was tiny and a disgrace to the category of canine.*
- *Middling and very ordinary.*
- *Celina was lucky to get away.*

She was seen as quite the heroine by now. As the stories were all so vague and unreal, she chuckled sometimes over it. But she always corrected these rumblings, her Walla Walla partner was the truest of dogs. Their need for a big story would have to look elsewhere. She could still hardly think of his name, without it hurting her throat in a place that only hurt when she wanted to cry.

A few local scroungers and strays would

gather around, bitching about her, saying she was 'spoiled goods' due to her foreign dalliance. She knew they really wanted to be her Walla Walla but shooting her down was the best option for now. And if you don't think a male dog can bitch, just watch his advances being rejected, Woah! Bite back!

One of them advanced on Celina. A raspy thin, wire-haired, bow-legged scoundrel. She rejected him. She had no need of a Walla Walla, hers was for life and was with Sebastian whether he was present or not. The raspy scoundrel became determined to destroy her.

She had known her own worst and her own best, there was nothing he could undermine her with. A typical scut, chasing the wheel of a car; he wouldn't know what to do with it when he caught up with it. Everyone knew he was full of hot air. Celina's lack of investment soon put his bravado in its place.

He took his frustrations elsewhere. The fight

was over before it began.

Celina continued to grow and flourish, she soared, and she roared.

Stop it!

Occasionally for exercise Celina would fly a little further afield, further than the confines of Saumur, further than it was necessary for exercise. She knew what she was doing, you're probably guessing what she was doing, but it needed a name and there was none. Each journey could be predicted, a little further, and a little further, and go on then, a little further. When she finally plucked up the courage to fly over St Joseph d'Andaines, she refused to look down, it was enough to be in its airspace.

She revisited it in this way several times and you know what is coming next, she eventually looked down with one of those eyes. You know those eyes that don't really look at their object but look in some vague vicinity of it – taking it in somehow, though details are scant.

The 'À Vendre' sign in the left downstairs window of Sebastian's house drove through her like a nasty bolt of compact thunder. She felt anger, she didn't know why. I suppose she did so much to get him home safely and clearly it wasn't enough. They were not coming back, and she would never know if he made it home or if he had recovered his health. That's all she wanted to know. Was he with them? Was he healthy? That would end it.

By now Celina had chicks of her own on the way. She knew she would settle in Saumur for life, but she also knew that the fittest of ducks could fly eight hundred kilometres and she couldn't help wondering how far Ireland was. She again contemplated perching herself on a ship bound for Ireland, but where then? It's a small island, but a bird of her difference will be noticed. She had heard of all sorts of stories of birds being captured by well-meaning humans and brought to what they call sanctuaries that they can't get out of. No, the risks were too high, but she desperately needed to see him, just see him, alive. Or if he was not alive, she needed to know.

Eight more fly overs, two with spring flowers, two with intense heat, two with yellowing leaves, and two with frosted windowpanes. The calendars of the years. The 'A Vendre' sign remained. The house was beginning to look broken down and neglected. Her visits were getting shorter and shorter as motherhood had demanded.

Things come to Pass, Not to Pause.

Celina continued to fly over St. Joseph d'Andaine whenever she could, until it brought about no sensation, no reaction, no change metabolic or otherwise. She began to wonder if the whole Walla Walla experience with Sebastian had actually happened. The further into the past it went, the more unreal it felt.

However, on one such visit, it was instantaneous, the recognition, the electric blue car. Her heart froze. She circled and landed, stumbled, gathered herself. Her vantage point perfectly picked for obscurity, a barn, its roof half caved in, nothing sensible would use it for cover.

Someone was inside the house at the left-hand downstairs window. They were removing the 'A Vendre' sign. New owners were coming perhaps. Jackie two legs and Sean two legs needed to clear out their belongings to make way for the new owners. The sign would be replaced by 'Vendu' any moment. She couldn't bear to see it.

Her frustration was palpable. There they were, Sebastian's human family. The Berners may be the adopted dog of Ireland, but they had a look of Switzerland about them. For one awful moment she wondered if he'd ended up in Switzerland. God help poor Sebastian, to lose himself in France, only to make it home and then be shipped off to Switzerland, how would he cope?

Next, Millie and Raven opened the back sliding doors, both with headphones on, they walked to the rear of the car. Millie popped the boot. And there it was, a black, white, and brown pup that was probably about ten weeks old, possibly twelve, but definitely no more than fourteen weeks. Celina's heart snapped as the little ball of fluff and energy walked from one end of the boot to the other to see exactly how he or she would dismount the chasm between the boot and the ground, without breaking a limb. Millie soon answered that one. She snatched the pup up in a one-armed scoop and the problem was solved, she dissolved into the house. Raven removed his headphones and went through a ritual of readiness, preparedness, carefulness. He looked worried. He reached into the boot and removed a lead, presumably for the pup, Celina thought. But there was something on the end of that lead, a little older, a lot plumper and a tad stiffer, Sebastian sniffed the French air knowingly and wistfully. The draught from the open car doors blew gently through his black lustrous fur and for a moment he looked like Aslan from Narina, all magical and majestic. He was a beast of such immense beauty. She almost forgot to breathe. The clock stopped. He was here. Alive, every muscle and sinew in his body was thriving.

It wasn't hard not to let him know she was there. It was the easiest thing in the world to watch him move and live and breathe and pant. So easy to shake and vibrate with joy not just for Sebastian, but for the Hegartys. They were a hotch-potch crew of perfection. A true family. It was easy for Celina to fly home.

Having been part of a Walla Walla was all she ever wanted but now she took up position here on the banks of the river in Saumur to be content, her chicks all around her as they watched the world go by. The world felt like her oyster. The jumper that she wore (a jumper that really belonged to her mother) often smelled like oysters, or so Celina was told. And when you know that the world is your oyster, ironically, you may prefer to stay put.

Sebastian still looked up to the belfry now and again, where he first saw Celina. He wondered if she would ever come back, he searched for her spirit in the constellations of the night sky. *Celina* he would say in doggery, *Selleena* the pup would say in mimicry as she waddled over to him in happy recognition of a name well chosen.

Of course, the Berners aren't for everyone, they're big, somewhat clumsy, and shed hideous amounts of hair. They are however, utterly adorable and the pup was just as gentle-natured as her father. She wore a cosy pink dog jumper in the evenings to help her in her youth against the wildness of the upper valley winds in this part of France and the bitterness of the winter to come in Ireland. Sebastian noticed a slight snag on the left-hand shoulder of her jumper. The tear was located where in warmer times Jackie's chasm of clipped neck fur would give Sebbie a cool reprieve. That chasm would forever remain a fond memory for Celina the duck.

Sebastian left it to fate whether this jumper on this particular Celina was really necessary. Some jumpers fit like a glove. Some jumpers are irritating and never feel quite right, some are gifts, and some are for occasional wear only. Either way, if you outgrow one of your own for whatever reason, snag it loose, and unravel yourself.

By now you're probably wondering who I am. My name is Moise, and I live next door. I have watched Celina and Sebastian from a distance over this entire episode. I'm somewhat moved by the bravery I've seen in both, it's a brokeny brave we don't often see these days. I think everyone has it in them to be brokeny brave, don't you?

I've travelled hither and tither to keep up with the story with a little help from my friends in neighbouring locations. You see my limit is six hectares, after that I quite lose my way. Anyway, I generally don't care much for dogs, ducks, and the like – they move too slowly to stir my instincts.

As our story now comes to an end, I bid you adieu so that I may bask for a time, in the kind evening sun. And as I prepare to, I am sure in this moment, that nothing could be more beautiful than the Loire in all seasons.

À plus tard, mes amis.

Glossary of Made-up Words

Brokeny: mended now, but not as it once was. Sometimes it is better.

Doggery: dog language.

Dolloping: behaving as though you are fed up.

Duckery: duck language.

Fallop: a fall with a particularly solid impact and a mono sound effect that does not reverberate.

Feck: an Irish phrase that means 'oh bother'.

Fouthered: attending to something clumsily (an Irish colloquialism).

Goodest: good cannot be made into a superlative.

Hoopa: a word you use to get you over a hurdle.

Stumpier: an enhancement of stumpy.

Swaggery: an enhancement of swagger.

Tinchy: a colloquial interpretation of the English word 'tincy' – meaning really small.

Welshy: an extension of the sound squelch.

Whimpery: we cannot add a 'y' to the word whimper, even though we just did.

Wooah: a sound you make when you're in trouble.

Lovely Old Phrases

Hotch Potch: a confusing mix.

Lickedy Split: very quickly (probably Scottish in origin).

N.B.

Jumper: European word for sweater.

Enjoy the French and Irish phrases, see if you can make out what they mean from the context of the sentence.

About the Author

Aisling Geraghty is a secondary school teacher of English and Religion. An avid dog lover, she has adopted four Bernese Mountain Dogs and many other dogs in need of a forever home, throughout her life. She lives in Bettystown, Co. Meath, Ireland with her husband, three children and two Berners Ezra and Sebastian.

Printed and bound by CPI Group (UK) Ltd, Croydon, CR0 4YY

01/06/2024

01010669-0004